# Amy's Disappearing Pickle

WRITTEN BY ELIZABETH CRARY ▪ ILLUSTRATED BY SUSAN AVISHAI

Parenting Press, Inc.

SEATTLE, WASHINGTON

**Parenting Press, Inc.**
P.O. Box 75267, Seattle, Washington 98125
www.ParentingPress.com

First edition
Printed in the United States of America

Book design by Margarite Hargrave

Library of Congress Cataloging-in-Publication Data
Crary, Elizabeth, 1942-
   Amy's disappearing pickle / written by Elizabeth Crary ; illustrated by Susan Avishai.
    p. cm. – (A kids can choose book)
   ISBN 1-884734-60-X (lib. bdg.) – ISBN 1-884734-59-6 (pbk.)
    1. Theft–Juvenile literature. 2. Problem solving in children–Juvenile literature.
   [1. Stealing. 2. Problem solving.] I. Avishai, Susan, ill. Title.

HQ784.S65 C73 2001
153.4'3–dc21
                                             00-062385

# Note to Parents, Teachers, and Caregivers

When a child faces a frustrating situation, the more ideas he or she considers, the more appropriate his or her behavior is likely to be.

---

The "Kids Can Choose" books model a process for solving problems and offer a variety of ways children can respond. Each book in this series explores a common problem for children, such as nonviolent teasing, theft of personal belongings, and personal space encroachment.

In each story some choices are successful and others are not–this helps children realize that they may need to try *several* strategies before they find one that works. The characters also model reflecting on various options *before they act*.

## How to Use These Books

Read the story and let your child make the choices. When you come to a box (■) read the question and wait while your child responds. Accept his or her responses without correction or criticism. You can ask your child to elaborate with questions like "Why do you think that worked?" or "Have you ever tried something like that?"

## Transition from Story to Real Life

It takes more than reading these books several times for children to be able to apply the principles to real life. Children need to practice using the approach in non-stressful situations. The following five steps make the transfer easier:

1. Act out the situation in the book with other kids or adults.
2. Brainstorm new ideas and add them to the list on page 30.
3. Pick five ideas (one for each finger) and act them out with an imaginary problem.
4. Choose five ideas for a past problem and act them out.
5. Ask your child to list different ways to handle a current problem and act them out.

When children can use the approach in non-stressful situations, you can remind them they have options in real life. For example, you could say, "What options have you considered?" or, for children who are reluctant to talk about their issues, "What might Amy have done in a situation like yours?"

Through these books you are helping your child learn to make smart decisions. Keep the tone light and *have fun!*

Elizabeth Crary
Seattle, Washington

Amy opened her lunch box cautiously. She wasn't sure what she would find. She hoped she would find a pickle, a juicy dill pickle like the ones the street vendor sold.

"Oh," she said disappointedly, "there's no pickle."

She took everything out of her lunch box, to be sure. Still, no pickle. Her pickle had disappeared again!

Yesterday and the day before she thought her dad had forgot to pack it. When she asked him, he said he packed the pickle as usual. So this morning, she watched him pack her lunch. She saw him slice the pickle in quarters the way she liked it, wrap it in foil, roll the ends, and put it in her lunch box.

"Where did it go?" she wondered. "It didn't get up and hop out," she reasoned, "so someone must have taken it out. But who would take my pickle?"

"Did you take my pickle?" she asked her friend Ellen.

"No," Ellen replied. Then she asked, "Why?"

"This is the third day it has disappeared out of my lunch box. It can't get out by itself, so somebody must have taken it."

"I saw Robin doing something by your locker this morning. Maybe she took it," Ellen volunteered.

"Hmm," Amy thought. "I remember her by my locker yesterday morning, too. Maybe she did take it. I'll demand she give it back."

"But what if she didn't take it?" Ellen asked.

"Oh, it would be terrible to accuse her. What can I do?" Amy moaned.

"We could spy on her," said Ellen, "or you could tell the teacher. Hey, maybe you could disguise the pickle," she laughed, imagining the pickle with sunglasses and a mustache.

"Or, I can ask my dad for ideas," Amy added. "He always tells me to look before I leap. That means I should think before I act."

■ What do you think Amy will try first?

*(Wait for child to respond after each question. Look at page 3, "Note to Parents, Teachers, and Caregivers," for ways to encourage children to think for themselves.)*

8

# 10  Ask the teacher for help

Amy was angry. She decided to ask her teacher for help.

She reviewed what her dad said about getting help: "Wait for a calm moment, then explain the facts." Amy waited until the kids started going out for recess, then she went to her teacher.

"Ms. Phillips, I have a problem and I don't know what to do," Amy explained. "Yesterday and the day before, my pickle was gone from my lunch box. I watched my dad put the pickle in this morning, and now it's gone too."

"That is a problem. Do you know who is taking your pickles?"

"I think so," Amy said.

"Well, I can't act without proof. However, you may put your pickle in my desk tomorrow, and I'll keep an eye on who goes to the lockers."

Amy was glad for Ms. Phillips's offer, but she wanted to do something.

■ What do you think Amy will try next?

# 12 Spy on Robin

"It won't do any good to spy on Robin now, since the pickle's gone. But we can watch the locker tomorrow," Amy said to her friends.

"Amy, tomorrow morning, wait until Ellen and I get to school before you go in. Then we can all take turns watching your locker," her friend Sara added.

That evening, Amy told her dad their plan. The next morning he packed a note with the pickle. When Amy got to school she left her lunch box in the locker. Ellen and Sara took turns watching, but no one went to Amy's locker.

The lunch bell rang. Amy noticed that Robin was not in her seat. She got up and hurried over to the lockers. Robin was standing by Amy's locker with a pickle-shaped package in her hand. "What are you doing?" Amy gasped angrily, as Ellen and Sara came up behind her.

"Nothing," said Robin, as she stepped back from the locker. Amy checked her lunch box. Her pickle was gone!

■ What do you think Amy will try next?

# 14 Demand Robin return her pickle

Amy recognized the special way her dad folded the foil. "Give me my pickle," she demanded.

"Why do you think it's your pickle?" Robin taunted.

"I know it is," Amy replied firmly, but she didn't say why.

"Besides," Ellen added, "someone's been taking pickles from Amy's lunch box. And you are standing in front of her locker with a pickle-shaped package in your hand."

"Well, she is standing in front of Lee's locker. Maybe she plans to take something from him," Robin retorted.

"Oh, no," Amy thought to herself, "this is not good. I know the pickle is mine, and I can prove it. Should I try to handle it alone and talk with Robin, or should I tell Ms. Phillips?"

■ What do you think Amy will try next?

# 16

# Talk to Robin

Amy decided she would try to handle things by herself. She asked Ellen and Sara to wait for her by the door.

Amy thought about what to say.

Finally she said, "Robin, I know the pickle is mine, and I can prove it. If you give me my pickle and promise not to take any more, I won't tell Ms. Phillips."

Robin looked at the package in her hand. She didn't see how Amy could prove it was her pickle, but she wasn't sure. Then she thought about how mad Ms. Phillips and her parents would be if they knew what she had done.

"Okay," Robin answered, "here's your stupid pickle."

"And the promise," Amy prompted.

"I promise I won't take any more pickles," Robin added.

*The End*

■ How do you like this ending?

# 18 Call the teacher

"Ellen, get Ms. Phillips," Amy ordered.

"Ms. Phillips, every morning, my dad packs me a pickle. Yesterday and the day before someone took the pickle from my lunch box. Robin is standing in front of my locker with my pickle in her hand!" exclaimed Amy.

"It's my pickle," Robin retorted. "I like pickles, too."

The teacher took the package. Looking at both girls, she asked, "How can we determine whose pickle this is?"

"My pickle has my name inside it," Amy stated.

Ms. Phillips opened the package. "So it does," she said. Then she asked, "Robin, what is our rule about taking things?"

"Ask first, and only take something if the person says it's okay," Robin mumbled.

"Now you must make amends to Amy," Ms. Phillips reminded Robin. "You may give her three pickles, pay her for the pickles, or do something else. What will you do?"

"Give her three pickles." Robin replied.

*The End*

■ How do you like this ending?

# Ask Dad for ideas

Amy stared blankly at her dinner plate. She wanted to tell her dad about her problem, but wasn't sure how to start.

"Dad," she said hesitantly, as she pushed her food around. "I have a problem. My pickles have been disappearing at school. I'm not sure what to do."

"Ah. Is that why you watched me so closely when I packed your lunch this morning?" he asked.

"Uh, huh. I thought you might be forgetting to pack a pickle," Amy replied. "But someone is taking them."

"That's a tough problem. You don't want more pickles to disappear, and you can't accuse someone unless you have proof. Would you like some ideas?" Dad asked. Amy nodded.

"Here are three ideas: You can hide the pickle so nobody can find it, do something unexpected, or decide it's no big deal."

■ What do you think Amy will try next?

# Hide the pickle

"Where can I hide my pickle so the Sneak can't find it?" Amy wondered. "If I hide it in my backpack, it will be easy to find. I think I need to make it look like something else. Where's a good place to hide a pickle?"

"I could use a fake book like Uncle Matt's," she thought. "It was hollow inside so you could hide things. But I don't know where to get one."

She picked up her crayon box. "I bet a pickle will fit in here if I take some colors out. But my crayons might get broken," she pondered.

"I know," she said, "I can use my old crayon box." She got the old box and showed it to her dad. "Look," she said, "I can take some old crayons out and my pickle will fit in here. The Sneak won't find it."

Amy's dad cut the pickle and wrapped it in foil. Amy slipped it into the crayon box. She was excited. Just before lunch she checked her backpack to see if the pickle was still in the crayon box. "Hurray!" she said to herself, "my pickle is still there."

*Turn to page 28.*

# 24 Decide it's no big deal

Later that night Amy was having a hard time settling down to sleep, even though Dad had read two chapters in *Charlotte's Web*. She was thinking about something he had once said.

"Dad, what does 'It's no big deal' mean?" Amy asked.

"Well," Dad answered thoughtfully, "It is deciding whether you want to fight or let go of the issue. For example, you can decide that eating a pickle at school doesn't matter to you — that you will eat your pickles at home, instead."

"But I should be able to eat pickles at school. That's not fair," Amy responded angrily.

"True, Amy, it's not fair. And, you need to decide how much it matters to you. And how you want to handle the situation," Dad explained.

"Well, I don't want people taking my pickles," Amy stated firmly. "But I don't mind eating them just at home," she added.

Amy thought for a bit, then turned to her dad, "I think I'll save my pickle for a snack when I get home."

*The End*

■ How do you like this ending?

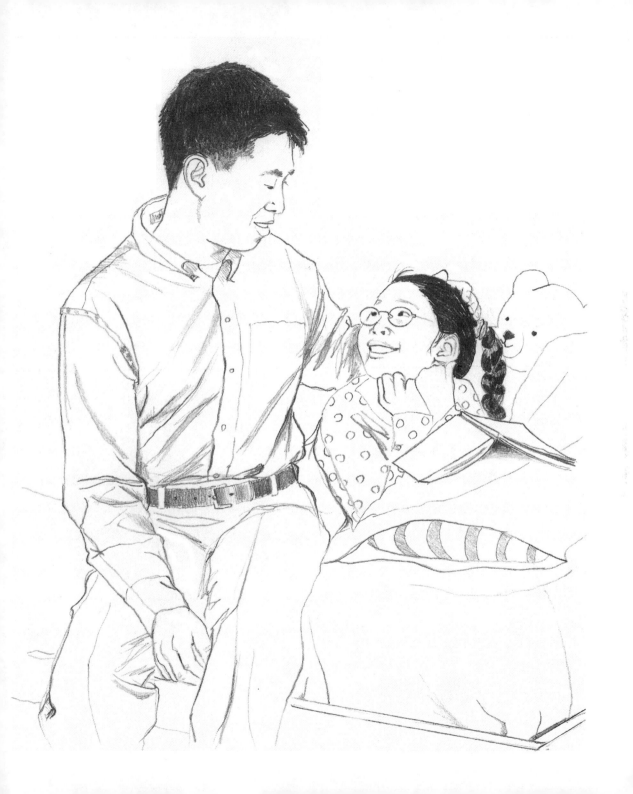

# 26 Do something unexpected

"What can I do that would be unexpected?" Amy asked herself.

"I could gift wrap the pickle. That would be unexpected, but I don't want to do that. Or I could give the Sneak two pickles, but I'd feel worse," she moaned. "Maybe I could make the Sneak think she's getting a pickle when she's not. That would be unexpected."

"Let's see, how can I make a fake pickle?" Amy wondered. "A wad of paper is too light and a banana is too nice. I know, I could use play dough," she thought excitedly.

Amy got out her play dough and made a green "pickle" and set it aside. Next she wrote a note, "Please eat your own pickles." Amy wrapped both in foil, just like her dad wrapped her pickles.

The next morning, she put the fake pickle in her lunch box and a real pickle in the bottom of her pack. At school, when she opened her lunch box, the fake pickle was gone. After that, her pickles never disappeared again!

*The End*

■ How do you like this ending?

Amy sat down at the table with Ellen. She spread her lunch out in front of her. Everything looked so yummy, especially her pickle! After eating her sandwich she savored every bite of her pickle. "Umm-umm, good," she said.

It was nice to have the disappearing pickle mystery solved. Now she didn't have to worry about her pickle anymore.

*The End*

■ How do you like this ending?

# Idea page

| Amy's ideas | Your ideas |
|---|---|
| Ask the teacher for help | ■ |
| Spy on Robin | ■ |
| Demand Robin return Amy's pickle | ■ |
| | ■ |
| Talk to Robin | ■ |
| Call the teacher | ■ |
| Ask Dad for ideas | ■ |
| Hide the pickle | ■ |
| Decide it's no big deal | ■ |
| Do something unexpected | ■ |
| | ■ |
| | ■ |
| | ■ |

# Solving social problems...

*Children's Problem Solving Books* teach children to think about their problems. Each interactive story allows the reader to choose the main character's actions and see what happens as a result. Useful with 3–8 years. 32 pages, illustrated. $6.95 each. Written by Elizabeth Crary, illustrated by Marina Megale.

# Solving interpersonal problems...

*Kids Can Choose Books* teach children to think about problems they may have with other children. Each interactive story allows the reader to choose the main character's actions and see what happens as a result. Useful with 5-10 years. 32 pages, illustrated. $7.95 each. Written by Elizabeth Crary, illustrated by Susan Avishai.

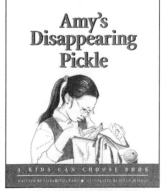

Someone is stealing Amy's pickle. What can she do?

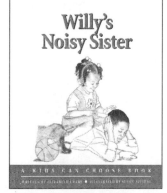

Willy needs some peace and quiet. His sister wants to play–NOW! What can he do?

One of Heidi's classmates always snatches her hat off her head. What can she do?

# Coping with intense feelings . . .

*Dealing with Feelings Books* acknowledge six intense feelings. Children discover safe and creative ways to express them. Each interactive story allows the reader to choose the main character's actions and see what happens as a result. Useful with 3-9 years. 32 pages, illustrated. $6.95 each. Written by Elizabeth Crary, illustrated by Jean Whitney.

# Facing life's challenges . . .

*The Decision Is Yours Books* offer realistic dilemmas commonly faced by young people. Readers choose from among several alternatives to solve the problem. If they don't like the result of one solution, they can try a different one. Useful with 7-11 years. 64 pages, illustrated. $5.95 each. Various authors, illustrated by Rebekah Strecker.

*Leader's Guide* ($14.95) written by Carl Bosch offers activities that allow children to talk about values, ethics, feelings, safety, problem solving, and understanding behavior.

Library-bound editions available. Call Parenting Press, Inc. at **1-800-992-6657** for information about these and other helpful books for children and adults.

*Prices subject to change without notice.*